I'm Getting Ready For Kindergarten

Written by B. Annye Rothenberg, Ph.D.
Child/Parent Psychologist

Illustrated by
Bonnie Bright

REDWOOD CITY, CALIFORNIA

DEDICATION

*To the many parents who do all they can — and then even more —
to raise their children well.
And to my son, Bret, who regularly inspires me to help parents
master the challenges and savor the joys of raising children —
and then reap the rewards when they're all grown up.*

—B.A.R.

*To Martha, who is about to start kindergarten, and to her big sister,
Libby, who I know will do a wonderful job of getting her ready.*

— B.B

Library of Congress Control Number: 2012924112
ISBN: 978-0-9790420-5-8 (pbk.)

Printed in China.   First printing May 2013
10 9 8 7 6 5 4 3 2 1

Published by
PERFECTING PARENTING PRESS
REDWOOD CITY, CALIFORNIA
www.PerfectingParentingPress.com

To order by phone, call:
(810) 388-9500 (M-F 9-5 ET)
For other questions, call:
(650) 275-3809 (M-F 8-5 PT)

Children's book in collaboration with
SuAnn and Kevin Kiser
Palo Alto, California

Parents' manual edited by
Caroline Grannan
San Francisco, California

Book design by
Cathleen O'Brien
San Francisco, California

• WHAT'S IN THIS BOOK FOR CHILDREN AND FOR PARENTS •

This sixth book in a series focuses on kindergarten readiness. Starting kindergarten is an important and exciting step for families. *During the year before kindergarten, children hear a lot about starting "big kids' " school, and they have many questions.* In the story for children, Jillian isn't sure she'll like kindergarten or that she'll be liked or even ready for all there is to learn. The story tells of her concerns and how her parents and preschool teachers help her become prepared *and* reassured.

As parents, most of us are happy and enthusiastic that our child is reaching this milestone, but we can also feel uncertain about our child's readiness. We know that reading and writing are now taught in kindergarten rather than beginning in first grade. Many parents have thought long and hard about whether their child needed another year before kindergarten (such as a year in pre-kindergarten or junior kindergarten). We wonder and worry about what we should do to prepare our child for *today's* kindergarten.

The Parents' Guidance Section of this book will help you determine what additional help your child will need from you to be ready for kindergarten and exactly how to help him[*]. The guidance section covers: helping your child learn to do what he's asked, how much he should be doing for himself, helping him to be academically ready, and the routines at home that make his day at school easier. It also provides useful guidance about emotional maturity and friendship skills, and about speech and motor skills. *The parent section is comprehensive, so it includes more than any individual family will need to work on.* Try not to be overwhelmed. *Look through the headings and the "Ask Yourself" questions under each of the 13 topics so you'll know which areas to work on with your child and how.* (This book will also help you decide if your child will need another year before starting kindergarten.)

Most kids eagerly anticipate starting kindergarten, ready to learn new things. Talking to your child and teaching him what he'll need to know will reduce your child's concerns and yours, and increase his skills and readiness. All this will make his adjustment to kindergarten smoother and happier.

— Annye Rothenberg, Ph.D., *Child/Parent Psychologist*

❖ *I'm Getting Ready for Kindergarten* is an outstanding guide for both parents and children. *Parents will learn how to thoroughly prepare their child for today's increased kindergarten demands.* In the story for children, youngsters will find their questions answered and their enthusiasm about the new world of kindergarten growing. I look forward to sharing this book with the families of my entering kindergarten students.
— Joyce Ottey, Kindergarten Teacher; Sutter Elementary School, Santa Clara, CA

[*] To avoid the awkward use of "he/she," the sections in this book will alternate between both.

One day I got a letter in the mail.

"Please read it to me, Mommy," I said.

"Dear Jillian," Mommy read, "I'm in kindergarten and I like it a lot. I will visit you soon. Your friend, Nirav."

"When will I get to go to kindergarten?" I asked.

"At the end of summer, Honey," said Mommy.

"Can I go too?" asked my little sister Molly.

4

"When you get bigger," said Mommy.

"Will I learn to write a letter in kindergarten, like Nirav?" I asked.

"I think so," said Mommy. "You can ask your teacher tomorrow."

5

The next day, at preschool, I asked my teacher, "What will we learn in kindergarten?"

"In kindergarten you'll learn how to read and write the letters of the alphabet and know the sounds they make," said Mrs. Chandler.

"T sounds like *tuh*," said Tyler. "It's the first letter in my name."

"That's right," said Mrs. Chandler. "You'll also learn a lot about numbers. To help you get ready for kindergarten, we're going to do some new projects."

"What kind of projects?" I asked.

"Projects with letters and numbers," said my teacher. "And coloring and cutting. I need everyone to do the projects at the same time."

"Why?" asked Adreana.

"So I can see if anyone needs help," said Mrs. Chandler.

"Will we still choose our own projects sometimes?" I asked.

"Yes," said Mrs. Chandler. "And we'll do many projects together. Let's do one now."

We did a project with letter shapes.

"This is fun," said Keisha.

I wanted to do puzzles instead.

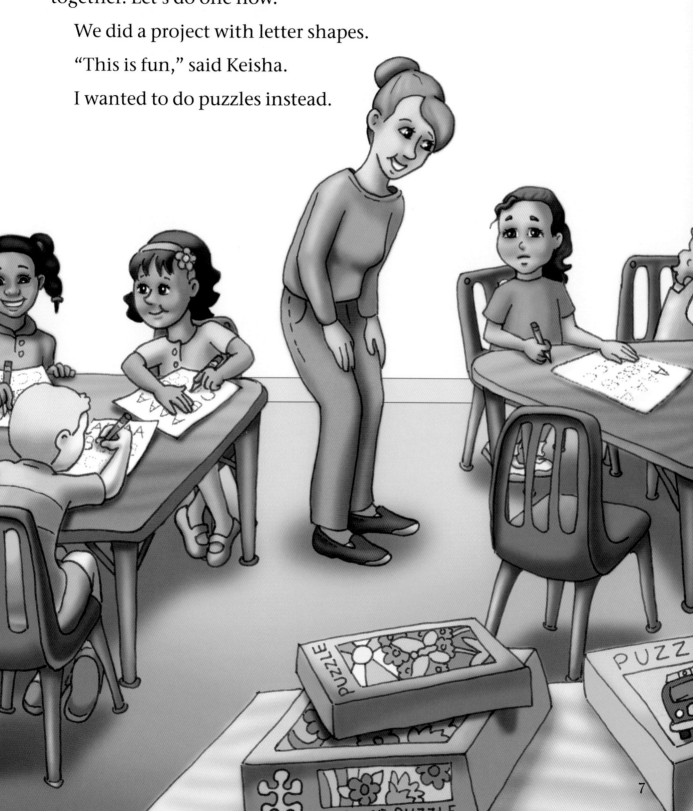

That evening, Daddy asked, "Jillian, how was school today?"

"Mrs. Chandler is helping us get ready for kindergarten. We all did a project at the same time so she could see who needed help."

"What a good idea," said Mommy.

"I liked preschool the way it was," I said. "I did things when I wanted to."

"You like story time and music time, and everybody does those at the same time," said Daddy.

"But why does preschool have to change?" I said. "I don't think I'm going to like it anymore."

"Then I don't like school anymore either," said Molly.

"Your school is fun," I said.

"My school *is* fun," said Molly.

The next morning, Mrs. Chandler had us all draw clouds. My cloud looked like a fluffy bear.

Later, we all did puzzles at the same time. Our teacher helped us, and we even helped each other.

When it was time for free play, I played with blocks. I liked doing projects with my friends just as much as choosing my own. If kindergarten was like this, it would be fun.

On Saturday, I asked Mommy and Daddy, "What does kindergarten look like?"

"I know!" said Molly. "It looks like a garden."

Everybody laughed.

"Let's go to the kindergarten so you can find out," said Daddy.

We walked to Beacon School and peeked in the window.

"Look at all those books," I said. "And all the tables and chairs, and the big desk."

A woman in the room smiled and waved at us.

"That must be the teacher," Daddy said.

The woman opened the door and said, "Hello, I'm Mrs. Wong."

"We're the Russells," said Mommy. "We're showing our older daughter what kindergarten looks like."

"What's your name?" Mrs. Wong asked me.

b Cc Dd Ee Ff Gg Hh Ii Jj Kk Ll

0 1 2 3 4 5 6 7 8 9

"I'm Jillian," I said. "I'm five years old and this is my sister Molly. She's almost three."

"Please come in and see my classroom," said Mrs. Wong.

Mrs. Wong showed us around her classroom. I liked the cubbies for backpacks, the kids' names taped to the tables, and the alphabet on the wall.

"Thank you," I said when we were ready to go.

"It was a pleasure to meet you and your family, Jillian," said Mrs. Wong.

We all waved goodbye.

We played in the playground for awhile.

"I think Mrs. Wong is nice," I said. "Will she be my kindergarten teacher?"

"We'll find out when school starts," said Daddy.

"Will my teacher like me?" I asked.

"Mrs. Wong already likes you," said Mommy, "but all the kindergarten teachers really like kids."

"And they love to teach them new things," said Daddy.

Daddy held my hand as we walked home. "Honey, yesterday we got a letter from Beacon School saying that when you start kindergarten your teacher will want you to know how to color inside the lines, cut with scissors, and use glue," said Daddy. "And how to print your name, and how some of the letters of the alphabet look and sound."

"Your teacher will also want you to finish your projects and clean up after yourself," said Mommy. "And to be quiet when she's talking and to leave the other kids alone when they're working."

"That's a lot to remember," I said.

"I'm going to write all those things down and draw a picture next to each one," Daddy said.

"And we're going to help you practice them so you're ready for kindergarten," said Mommy.

Later, my friend Nirav and his mom came to visit.

"What do you do in kindergarten?" I asked Nirav as we played trains.

"I'm learning how to read and write," he said.

"Would you show me?" I asked.

"Sure," he said. He picked up one of my books. "***Why Do I Have To?***," he read. Then he wrote it too.

"That's good!" I said. "Do you like reading and writing?"

"I sure do," said Nirav. "Sometimes it's hard, but then my teacher helps me figure it out. There's lots of work in kindergarten, but it's fun too."

16

That night, Daddy showed me the list of things
that I should be ready to do when I start kindergarten.
I couldn't read it yet, but I liked Daddy's pictures.

Color inside the lines
Cut with scissors
Use glue
Print "Jillian"
Know some letter sounds & shapes
Listen to the teacher
Finish your projects
Clean up after yourself
Be quiet when the teacher is
Don't interrupt other children

Soon preschool ended and summer started. Almost every day, Mommy and Daddy helped me get better at listening and cleaning up and not interrupting when other people talked. And they helped me learn more alphabet letters and the sounds they make.

At the end of summer, it was time for my first day of kindergarten at Beacon School. I wore new clothes and shoes and Mommy helped me put on my pink backpack.

I was still a little worried when Mommy and I got to kindergarten.

"I don't know if I'm ready," I said.

Mommy gave me a kiss for good luck.

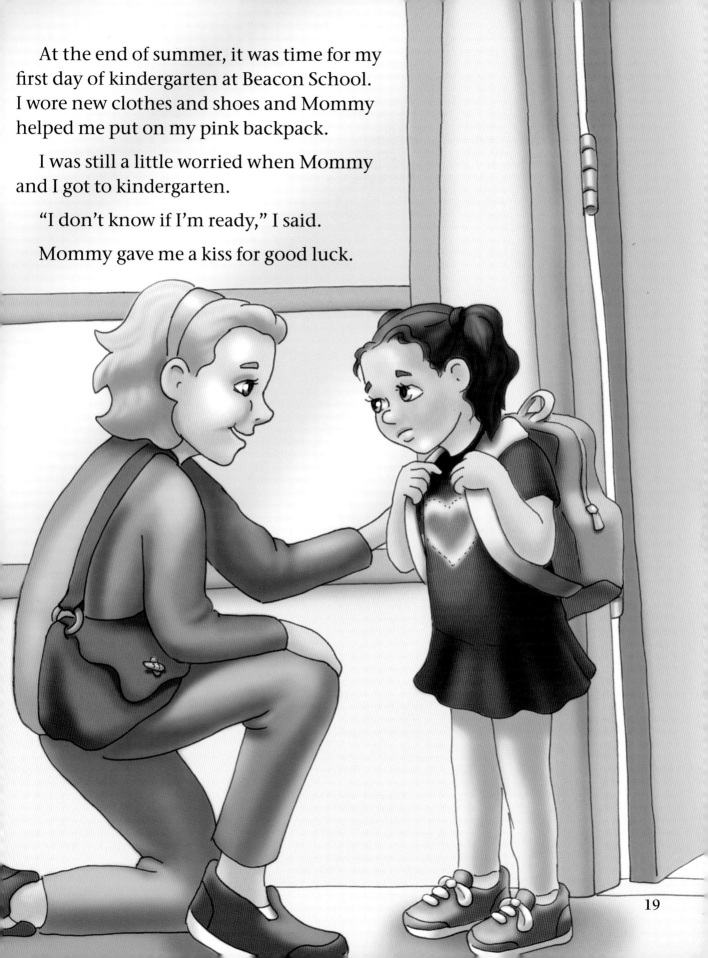

When I saw my new teacher, I was very happy. "Mrs. Wong!" I said.

"Hello, Jillian," said Mrs. Wong. "It's nice to see you again." She showed me my cubby and where I would sit, between Emma and Daniel.

There was a lot to learn on the first day of kindergarten. We started learning each other's names. We learned where everything is kept and where the kindergarten bathroom is. We learned that when Mrs. Wong claps her hands two times she wants us to be quiet. I even learned that my teacher's favorite color is the same as mine—pink!

After school, Mommy hugged me and asked, "How was your first day of kindergarten?"

"It was good," I said. "I made lots of new friends, and I don't feel worried anymore."

Molly handed me a pretty flower. "Were you ready for kindergarten today?" she asked.

"I was all ready for kindergarten," I said, "and I really liked it."

"Then I want to go too," said Molly, "...when I get bigger!"

"When you're big enough," I said, "I'll help you get ready for kindergarten!"

I learned new things every day in kindergarten, and by spring, with a little help, I wrote my very first letter.

"Dear Nirav, Kindergarten is fun, and I like it a lot too, just like you. Your friend, Jillian."

A GUIDANCE SECTION FOR PARENTS

• INTRODUCTION •

In many ways, sending our children off to kindergarten is the culmination of all of our child rearing. *Many parents wonder whether our children will know what they need to, will listen to their teachers, and will make friends.* Some of us may be concerned that they will have trouble separating from us. We're even more inclined to worry if our children have had difficulties in preschool – especially if they haven't been resolved.

This book has two goals: first, to help you know what your preschooler might wonder or worry about, so you can answer her questions and reassure her; *and second, to give you very specific guidance about what your child needs to know so she can be ready for kindergarten.* The children's story teaches both your child and you, while the parent guidance section is for you and any other caregivers your child has. Together, they provide the direction, skills, and confidence you need in preparing your child to thrive in kindergarten. It will also be useful to you in the first months of your child's kindergarten experience.

Kindergarten has changed over the last few years throughout the U.S. Today's parents remember kindergarten as having lots of playtime and being about three hours long. Reading and writing weren't taught until first grade. *The curriculum demands of kindergarten now throughout U.S. schools are much greater.* Although kindergarten curriculum goals for public schools are set by each state's department of education, most states have adopted a new guideline: the Common Core State Standards in language arts and math. Children begin learning to read, write, and do arithmetic in the autumn of the kindergarten year. To accommodate all this, most kindergarten days are at least four hours – some five and even six. Many subjects are taught in interesting ways, including more hands-on learning. *Kindergarten teachers give the children movement time – singing, wiggling and stretching breaks several times a day, along with recess – to make it easier for children to stay focused during their work time.*

The age for starting kindergarten is shifting. Most states now require children to be five to start kindergarten – by September 1 in some states and as early as June 1 in others. With greater curriculum expectations and longer school days, it makes sense to require that kindergartners be older. *Many schools will provide a list of expected skills for entering kindergartners. Make sure you ask for the list and use it to guide your child's preparation.* It will probably include behavioral and academic areas. You really should *do more rather than less* in preparing your child. Many educators *unintentionally underestimate* what children should know before they start kindergarten. If their classmates are more prepared than they are, children easily get discouraged about school, and it can be hard for them to change their view.

Enrolling a kindergarten-age child in a pre-kindergarten or junior kindergarten can be especially useful if your child has challenges in areas such as social or emotional maturity, has difficulty doing what she's asked, has a short attention span, is very fidgety and active, or has speech or fine motor delays. *Your child can benefit by waiting a year to attend kindergarten if she will be stressed by having to work harder than most of her classmates to keep up with them.*

Some elementary schools assess the child's kindergarten readiness to help the parents decide whether to send the child to kindergarten or wait another year, and/ or to help the school place the child in the best classroom for her. (**Public** schools can make recommendations as to whether the child should or shouldn't start K, but parents typically are entitled to make the final decision.) It can be helpful to get your child's preschool teacher's opinion. You may also want to meet with the school principal or kindergarten teacher in the spring to hear their views. *This book can also help you make this decision, especially if your child seems behind in many areas.*

During the school year, the kindergarten teacher will assess the child's progress regularly and report to the parents. There are parent-teacher conferences in autumn and sometimes in the spring. You can also meet with the teacher at other times as needed. In kindergarten, the children are usually expected to work on the same activity at the same time, unlike preschool, where the children often choose many of their own activities. ***Kindergarten teachers work very hard – especially at the beginning of the school year – to help the children get used to kindergarten, no matter whether they came from a play-based preschool or a more academic one.***[1] Make sure you take your child to see the kindergarten at her new school, especially if it takes her a while to adapt to new situations. It would be good to visit when the teacher is available for a few minutes.

Parents also need to take a bigger role in helping

prepare their children for kindergarten. Although some of our children still won't be as ready as we'd like them to be, at least we will have provided additional social, emotional, and academic training to them, ***before*** and ***as*** they begin kindergarten. ***It pays for parents to get involved in their child's learning before she starts kindergarten***, and to be prepared to help her as needed during her kindergarten year and beyond. ***The following three sections show a complete set of topics. Try not to get overwhelmed. Pick one topic to work on at a time. As you turn to each topic, read the "Ask Yourself" questions so you'll know in what areas your child might need help and how to help her.***

---

[1]Make sure your child has had some group experience where she needs to do what the teacher or coach says — before she starts kindergarten.

SECTION ONE
Guiding Your Child: Three through Five Years

1. Teaching Your Child to Listen to You and Other Adults (see pp. 28-29) • *getting cooperation* • *using the best consequences*

2. What Guidelines at Home Will Help Your Child to Be Ready to Learn at School (see pp. 29-30) • *routines* • *exercise* • *TV and other screen time* • *food, etc.*

3. What Should Children Be Able to Do for Themselves? (see pp. 30-31) • *dressing* • *washing* • *cleaning up, etc.*

4. What Should Children Do for the Family? (see pp. 31-32) • *the benefit of doing chores* • *how to get started*

5. Guiding Your Child's Emotional Maturity (see pp. 32-35) • *separation issues* • *learning to handle frustration* • *difficult feelings*

6. Guiding Your Child's Social Maturity (see pp. 35-37) • *friendliness* • *compromising and negotiating* • *accepting rules* • *seeing others' perspectives* • *learning right from wrong, etc.*

SECTION TWO
Guiding Your Child: Four Through Five Years (Pre-K)

7. Your Child's Speech and Language Readiness (see pp. 37-39)
• *listening and understanding*
• *expressing himself in a group*

8. Your Child's Fine and Gross Motor Readiness (see pp. 39-41)
• *printing* • *coloring, cutting, gluing*
• *drawing* • *running, galloping, etc.*

9. Preparing Your Child Academically for Kindergarten (see pp. 41-43)
• *how to encourage reading* • *teaching letters, numbers, shapes etc.*

10. Preparing Your Child for the Structure of Kindergarten (see p. 43) • *working independently* • *speaking up* • *handling transitions*

SECTION THREE
Guiding Your Child As Kindergarten Begins: Five through Six Years

11. Preparing Your Kindergartner to Be Able to Focus on the Schoolwork (see pp. 44-45) • *practicing following directions* • *sticking with schoolwork* • *problem-solving*

12. What's a Good Daily Routine for Your Kindergartner? (see p. 45)
• *making before-school time calmer*
• *good approaches for after school*

13. Working with Your Child's Kindergarten Teacher (see p. 46)
• *ways to communicate*
• *benefiting from the teacher's advice*

• SECTION ONE •

GUIDING YOUR CHILD: THREE THROUGH FIVE YEARS

1. Teaching Your Child to Listen to You and Other Adults

ASK YOURSELF: *Does my child usually do what we (and other adults) tell him to do … without our having to tell him over and over? If not, what can we do about it now?*

Since your child will be expected to do what the teacher says, this is the first thing to look at. Getting our children to do what we ask is a cornerstone in child-rearing. Parents are the representatives of society for our children. What we teach our kids to do at home, they'll do elsewhere; what we let them get away with at home is what they expect to get away with elsewhere. Although children may behave better with their teachers than they do with their parents, it's still essential that our children learn to respect our rules. Disrespectful behavior means our children will annoy others and be corrected a lot. Then teachers may find him difficult to work with.

• **Does your child get too much say?** Many families are giving their young children too much say, such as asking their three-year-old, "What restaurant do you want to eat at?" Too much say too young makes children feel they should have more authority than is reasonable. Give your child choices that affect only him – "apple or pear for lunch?" – not those that affect you, such as whether to go to the cleaners or the shoe store first, or what to make for dinner. Too much say makes children more demanding over time instead of less.

• **Teach your child early on to talk to you with respect.** Teach him to say, "Mom (Dad), when you have a minute, can you please..." *If* you think your child seems entitled and angry when he doesn't get to decide, the book *Mommy And Daddy Are Always Supposed To Say Yes ... Aren't They?* by this author covers this topic with a story for young children and guidance for parents.

• **Make it fun for preschoolers to listen:** Preschoolers are naturally oppositional. Logic and reasoning are not the best tools to use with preschoolers. When parents try logic such as "You played with the toys, so you need to pick them up and put them away," youngsters often don't comply. *It is very helpful to make your requests – about half the time – sound fun and/or interesting.* Here's an example using bathtime: "Pretty soon, it's going to be time to get a paper cup and put some holes in it so you can take it into your bath." *We want to make it easier for our preschoolers to cooperate without battles.* It's true that it does take more effort to come up with fun ideas, but when this results in a more receptive child, there's less stress in the family. If we don't make it easier, they often don't cooperate or comply, and they end up getting a consequence. It's worse when parents back down. When you ask your child to put his toys away and he ignores and refuses, it's tempting to let it go and put the toys away yourself, or leave them out and try again later. That makes a child more likely to believe he doesn't have to do what adults say. If you feel ambivalent about telling your child what to do, remind yourself of the reasons behind your request. Then you'll be less likely to cave in when he tests your limits by arguing, refusing, or ignoring. If you give concessions, he'll test you more and respect you less – and may respect other adults less, such as his teachers.

• **Effective consequences:** Besides using more fun and interesting ways to motivate your child to do what you ask, it's essential to use effective consequences. *Consequences should cause even a young child to think twice before he repeats the misbehavior.* Consequences should help your child be less impulsive and develop more self-control or inner discipline. It's not acceptable anymore to use consequences that hurt, frighten, or humiliate children. Consequences can be effective and memorable if they're boring and tedious. The most common consequences are some form of time-out and some form of take-aways, such as taking away dessert, electronic devices, etc. But we need more than just two types of consequences. If you have only time-outs and take-aways, your child is likely to start saying, "I like time-out. I want to stay in time-out" or, "I don't care if you take my Legos away. I didn't want them anyhow." You're left to wonder if he means it, and if so, what consequences you have left. *When we have more than just two types of consequences, it's harder for children to anticipate which one we'll use and then prevent us from doing our parenting job.* Here are three other types of consequences:

Wasted time. When we have to tell our kids over and over, especially if we're already using ways to make it easy for children to cooperate, we should let them know: "There has not been enough good listening, and now I'm behind in all the things I have to do, so I won't have time to cook with you." This consequence helps them understand that they will lose out on something they want – time with you.

Practicing better behavior. When your child is rude, ignores you, hurts his sibling, etc., tell and/or show him a better way to behave. Just telling him what to do differently next time – "I don't ever want you to do that again" – rarely changes a child's behavior. Have him try the better behavior once and then practice it two or three more times. Don't just tell preschoolers to use their words; give them the words. Practicing the better behavior helps a child internalize it, and this makes him more likely to behave next time.

Expressing empathy: Ask your child, "What am I thinking (or feeling) about you right now, and why am I thinking (feeling) that?" After a few times with a child four years or older, have him tell you *two* things you're thinking. Let him know you'll decide if he has given a good enough answer. It's good for children to be able to look at their behavior through our eyes.

For a story for youngsters on why parents have rules, and a parent guidance section on how preschoolers think, how to get them to do what you ask, and details on these new consequences, see the book **Why Do I Have To?** by this author.

• **To be most effective:** Many parents tell their child to do something three, four, five, or more times and threaten consequences but don't actually use them – sometimes until the parent is very angry, probably screaming. *This teaches the child that he doesn't have to listen until he's been told over and over. It would be much more effective to start your consequences after one warning. Otherwise we are inadvertently training our child not to listen until we get angry.* Try not to bribe your child with things (junk food, toys, money) for good behavior. We don't want to "pay" him to behave. Teach him to want to please you because he sees how happy you are, how positive you are with him, and how much more time you have to spend with him.

• **Explain your role:** Lots of young children think that parents have rules and consequences because parents are mean *and* don't want them to have fun. Make sure you tell them, *"It's a mom and dad's job to teach you everything five- (or six-)year-olds need to know about how to behave."* Tell them that even if you are tired or busy, or just don't want to, you still have to teach them many things. Use examples like getting dressed, learning about healthy foods, cleaning up toys, washing themselves in the bathtub, etc., so they realize what you've been helping them learn. Their job is to learn what you're teaching. Use an appropriate opportunity to remind them that they'll be going to kindergarten soon, and you will help them by answering their questions about kindergarten. And, along with their preschool teachers, you'll be teaching them the things they need to know to be more ready for kindergarten.

2. What Guidelines at Home will Help Your Child Be Ready to Learn at School?

ASK YOURSELF: *Do I know the daily routines kids need, including how much sleep and exercise she needs? What are the best ways for her to spend her time after her day in kindergarten?*

• Make sure you have **set routines that occur at regular times** each day, such as getting dressed, mealtimes,

TV (if any), toy pickup, bathtime, and bedtime. Regular routines help a child know what's expected and be more willing to comply. Without routines for all the daily expected activities, children test the limits more. *In addition to routines' making home life more agreeable, they help children accept daily school expectations* such as putting backpacks away, cleaning up their work space, and listening to the bell when recess is over.

• Especially in the first half of the school year, *schedule your kids into very few activities beyond the school day,* because the demands of kindergarten are often exhausting for children.

• *A regular bedtime* makes it much easier for your children to fall asleep faster. Younger kids need more sleep – five-year-olds as much as 11 hours a night, six-year-olds 10 to 11 hours. This means bedtime around 8 to 8:30 p.m., with kids getting up about 6:30-7 a.m. *Make sure you don't regularly wake your children in the morning.* If they don't wake up on their own, it means they're not getting enough sleep. They are still growing and developing and don't do well if they haven't had all the sleep they need. (If necessary, move your child's bedtime back about 15 minutes, and after a few days, move it back 15 more minutes.)

• A minimum of an hour a day of *heart-pounding exercise is essential. This includes* running around, kicking a soccer ball, biking, jumping, e.g. on a *mini-trampoline;* basically, moving fast. Some children who are very high-energy and find it hard to sit still long enough in school will do much better having 10 or 15 minutes of running around (at home or at school) before they start their school day. (If your child needs lots of exercise, find out if she's being active or not during outdoor time.) Also, if your child's not active enough on her own, add exercise into your family time. When she's adjusted to the demands of kindergarten, you can schedule some additional activities for her, including active ones if she needs them.

• If your child has a long school day (five hours or more), eliminate *television* from the daily routine. There are better ways for your child to relax. Children need time to be with you after they've been in a group all day – talking, playing with you, even working **with** you on chores. And they need time to follow their own interests and/or be with sibs and neighborhood kids.

TV is a mesmerizing and sedentary type of activity, although some shows do aid learning and are worthwhile entertainment. Parents know that they have to limit TV viewing and typically have rules, such as TV only on weekends for an hour. When there is a short school day, a half hour is reasonable.

• Parents also need to establish limits on the *other types of screen time*, including video games, computers, smart phones, and tablets. Of course, some of these activities are valuable, and they are more interactive than TV, *but the more we allow children to be occupied with them, the less able they will be to find other things to do.* Then children may prefer them *even when we're available*, because they can become addictive. Your child can accept the limits if there is something very interesting to do right after her electronics time, such as playing ball outside or planning something with you. A half hour a day of screen time would be the recommendation. If your young child has a busy and long day, the best guideline is *no* electronics time on weekdays.

• Remember to keep teaching your child about **healthy food.** She needs that to have enough stamina for the day and to build the foundation for a healthy body and a healthy life. Check in with the school so you can see if the kids have enough adult supervision to actually eat their morning snack and their lunch[2] rather than throwing them in the garbage. (It's useful for parents to see what comes home uneaten.) Check to see if the school's staff has rules about eating the healthier food first and not allowing children to give each other food. For a story for kids and guidance for parents about healthy eating, see *I Like To Eat Treats* by this author.

3. What Should Children Be Able to Do for Themselves?

ASK YOURSELF: *Am I expecting what I should from my child in all the essentials for his age – dressing, bathing, grooming, eating, toileting, cleaning up after himself, sleep, etc.?*

Kindergartners are expected to be quite self-sufficient. The skills described here are part of developing self-sufficiency. *As you read through this section, mark*

---

[2]Depending on the school and situation, some children buy the school lunch rather than bringing a lunch from home.

his teeth, though he'll probably need help to do it well till he's about seven. Blow his nose with some skill.

• *go without naps*, be able to fall asleep on his own, and sleep through the night except when sick or scared.

• help out with younger siblings.

• shop with you without typically demanding and tantrumming that you buy toys and treats for him.

He should also **know his whole name, his parents' names,** his street address, **and the phone number that's the best way to reach the most available parent**. You may also want to teach him about using 911, but make clear to him that it's only to be used in an emergency, and why that is.

Your child will feel more confident and secure if he can do what children his age are typically capable of. It's best to avoid doing too much for him even though we can do the jobs faster and better. There's much we need our children to learn to do for themselves, and it's best that we teach it at an age-appropriate time. We don't want to still be teaching hand-washing to seven-year-olds, or reminding eight-year-olds to say "please" and "thank you."

4. What Should Your Children Do for the Family?

ASK YOURSELF: *What's the value in having our children do chores for the family, and what chores are age-appropriate?*

Usually, young children up through age five want to imitate what we do. They are eager to try any chore and find all of them great fun. But by age six or seven, youngsters start looking at these activities (like clearing the table, or dumping garbage) as work. *Although you may feel your children shouldn't have household responsibilities, kids who help out at home find it easier to comply with all the "have-tos" at school.* There are many benefits to having children shoulder their share of the household work.

• Doing chores together helps build the spirit of "family," enabling kids to see that everyone has to do his share.

• *Children learn their parents' standards and work ethic when their parents teach them to do chores.* We

the skills your child still needs to work on. If he needs to work on many of these, **start with just one or two that can help him most at school**, and then add one or two more, etc. Start with cleanup skills. Then make sure he can get his clothes on and off and use the toilet at school.

By the time he starts kindergarten, your child should be able to:

• select his clothes, although you'll need to provide guidance for unexpected weather. Dress and undress himself, except for tying his shoes, difficult zippers, and snaps.

• *wash himself in the bath,* know how to put shampoo in his hair, wash his hands, and be completely toilet trained[3].

• *wash his hands* and do some food preparation, know about healthy eating, feed himself, stay at the table to eat, clear his plate and cup, and put his trash in the garbage.

• *put away his toys*, pick up his dirty clothes, help pack his backpack, and carry most of his own things into school and back to the car or home.

• *brush/comb his hair*, unless it's very difficult. Brush

---

[3]For toilet issues, see *I Don't Want To Go To The Toilet*, by this author.

don't want our children to learn to take the easy way out and do chores in a halfhearted way. Too many parents find that their school-age children who aren't motivated to do chores also won't try their best at schoolwork, sports, projects, etc.

• Getting kids accustomed to doing chores helps them learn patience and perseverance. You'll be able to see the results when your child readily accepts the structure and demands of kindergarten.

• Chores help children realize that doing ordinary and even tedious tasks are part of life, which helps them appreciate the activities that are fun and amusing.

There are many jobs that five- and six-year-olds can do regularly. Seven days a week is best, so they don't argue and negotiate with you every Monday because they didn't have chores on the weekend. Most of the jobs should take about five minutes. One or two regular jobs a day is reasonable. Teach your kids how to do the jobs. Try to do yours at the same time. In the kitchen, they can do such tasks as setting the table and rinsing dishes. They can empty wastebaskets and sort recycling. They can help with laundry and vacuum. Pet-care chores also teach compassion. Cooking probably shouldn't count, because most kids like it. Every month or two, have the kids look at your master list of chores. Offer them the chance to keep them, to trade jobs with their siblings, or to choose new ones. Doing chores is more interesting when they get to do something new, and it allows parents to teach kids more skills.

5. Guiding Your Child's Emotional Maturity

ASK YOURSELF: *Does my child depend on me too much? Does he get frustrated a lot? Does he have difficulty controlling his feelings?*

Kindergarten teachers consider emotional and social readiness very important. Several aspects of emotional maturity are important in your child's development and for his comfort in kindergarten and beyond.

The first aspect of emotional maturity is being able to separate from you. Kids need emotional independence to navigate through their kindergarten day. Most young children functioned comfortably in preschool without their parents and learned to depend on their teacher for guidance, direction, and reassurance. Most youngsters have also been cared for by sitters (or nannies). Children need enough of these experiences before kindergarten to feel confident that they can depend on their teacher in place of their parents.

However, in some families, the children may have spent most of their time with parents or relatives and have little experience being away from them. Often those children feel comfortable and emotionally supported only when with their family. These children may only want playdates at their home or want their parents to stay when they're at playdates or birthday parties. These children only want to be with adults who know their needs. Being with their parents makes their life so comfortable that they may feel uncertain when they're not with their family.

If your child seems too dependent on you, here are some things you can do:

• Teach your child a rhythm at home of together, apart, together, apart. The "apart" refers to regularly encouraging your child to do some things on his own at home as you, the parent, are doing things on your own.

• Discourage your child from giving you orders by not responding to his directives like "You get it for me" or complying when he tries to tell you what to say when you're playing with him.

• Encourage your youngster to do as many things for himself as he's capable of – dressing himself, cleaning up his toys, and walking up the stairs rather than asking to be carried. When they see that they can do what other kids do, children feel more capable.

• Encourage your child to stay where he is, doing something on his own, when you leave the room briefly. Tell him where you're going and how quickly you'll be back ("I'm going to the garage, and I'll be back in a couple of minutes"), and suggest something he can do right where he is, if he isn't already engaged in something.

• Make sure your child can count on your word by being home when you say you will, picking him up on time, and regularly saying goodbye. *Children feel more secure and confident when they can depend on their parents' promises.* For a child to comfortably accept that he can count on his kindergarten teacher, he also needs

If a child's block building falls down or his friend can't come for a playdate, he experiences disappointment, sadness, and anger. On his own, he often can't find effective ways to move on and calm himself down. Young children therefore often have strong emotional outbursts that can be very upsetting to deal with. *But we create problems if we make a priority of trying to eliminate our kids' frustration to head off their tantrums.*

• *Allow him to be frustrated:* Children need to experience common frustrations. Be sure that you don't avoid limits or give concessions, just to avoid upsetting your child. When our child's block tower falls down, if we rebuild it for him, we're not allowing him to experience ordinary frustration. When he's annoyed with his lack of skill, we want to offer pointers and encouragement, but not give him the finished project.

• *Experiencing frustration:* Children also need to learn to cope with frustration when you set limits. For example, you tell him that the TV is going off at the end of this program. Then comes the time. He has a major meltdown as he screams for more television. You tell him he can watch one more show but then he really has to shut it off or else you will. This is a mistaken effort to prevent him from experiencing natural daily frustration. The TV needs to be shut off at the end of the program, as you said.

• *Don't cave in because …* If we give him his favorite food when it's not what the family is having, or read him another story after telling him "only one," this prevents a child from developing skill at handling frustration. Then he will usually respond angrily because he doesn't have enough experience accepting frustration and knowing that he'll feel OK in a minute.

• *Coping mechanisms:* Parents need to teach their kids *how to deal with frustration.* You can tell them about something that caused you frustration, how you felt, and some of the things you said to yourself. Children like to hear our stories and they need to know that not everything works out easily, even for an adult. When his blocks fall, he may say: "My bridge never stays up. I'm not doing blocks anymore." We can help by being empathetic: "Building is really frustrating today. Do you want to take a break or have some help?" If your child says no and gets even angrier, you can say, "Just thinking about blocks is making you furious. Let's try some-

to have had enough good experiences with teachers. His parents need to have expected and taught age-appropriate independence, and to have dependably kept promises they made to their children.

The second aspect of emotional maturity is to teach your child to deal with frustration. Frustration is a natural part of everyone's daily experience when things don't go the way we wanted or expected. For adults, that could be being stuck in a traffic jam. For children it could be that their block building fell. Frustration can come from being prevented from having what they want or from their own lack of skills.

Children hear "no" in their lives much more frequently than adults do. Parents have to say no, which is usually frustrating for kids. *Examples of things that frustrate kids are having to pick up their toys, not having things bought for them at every store, and having to shut off the TV. It's helpful for children to experience these common and necessary frustrations so they get used to coping when things can't be their way.* Adults are better able to handle the frustrations in our lives because we can usually understand why they're happening *and* because we have ways to calm ourselves down.

thing else." You can also teach him words to say when he's frustrated. It's best for him to know you understand his frustration and that there are options besides feeling stuck and angry.

• **Explain why the answer is no:** Give your child experience handling the frustration that's caused by our rules as well as by his own limited skills. Prepare him in advance. If you anticipate that he'll want something at the store and you don't plan to buy him anything, explain before you go into the store. Talking about reasonable expectations on your part and his own can be helpful. **Be ready to help him know what he can say to calm himself down.** "I can't get anything at the store today. But Daddy said he'll write what I want on a list and when we go to the store next Saturday, we'll look at the list and find one thing I can get." **When kids have to delay their impulses for a while, it helps them deal with frustration.**

The third aspect of emotional maturity is the skill of self-control. Teachers expect children by kindergarten age to be able to calm down quickly. They expect that a child who is dissatisfied with what he's drawing or writing won't rip up his paper, refuse to keep working, or start sobbing – or that he won't resist doing his schoolwork because he lost a game at recess. Kindergartners are expected to have more emotional control than preschoolers. Certainly, some children are much more emotionally intense than others, but parents can help their children control their overreactions.

• **Accepting feelings:** Parents should expect their children to have mild to strong feelings throughout the day, some positive and some negative. Most parents want to help their children with feelings. **Comments like "Just get over it," "Stop acting like a baby," "That's nothing to be upset about," or "If you don't stop it, you're getting a time-out" are not the best reaction to your child's difficult feelings.**

• **Give him the words to use:** It would be better to acknowledge our kids' strong feelings with, "Of course you're mad. You wanted Tyler to come over for a play-date, but he can't because you have karate." This allows and encourages your child to express his upset feelings. Then you can teach him what words he could use. If he's mad at you, suggest that he say: "Mom, I'm mad at you

because Tyler couldn't come over." Then tell him what's coming next: "Let's go home and make your snack and play for a little while before karate." And finally, plan with him for a playdate with Tyler soon.

• **Words, not meltdowns:** We want to teach our children how to express difficult feelings in words instead of out-bursts. This is part of maturing from preschool age to kindergarten age. Teach them how to talk to themselves if they get upset easily. **Most youngsters can't just "calm down" when we tell them to. Youngsters benefit from being able to express their feelings in words. They can learn that when they use their words, we understand why they're upset.** Some children can calm down just from a change of scene such as going to their room and playing, building, or looking at books. Other children need more help.

• **Self-talk:** You can start teaching your child about "self-talk," also known as inner dialogue. Tell your children about things in your day that upset you, and **share some of the things you said to yourself that made you more upset and the things that calmed you down,** including how you got yourself to think of something else. Help your child learn the thoughts and words that help him calm down faster.

• **Suggest words:** Start giving your preschooler the actual words to talk to himself about his difficult emotions. As children get to be about six years old, they'll get better at talking to themselves – especially if you began teaching self-talk to them in their preschool years. Teach him to tell himself: "I'm so mad that I have to come in for dinner now. I'm going to tell Mom I'm mad at her. That'll make me feel better. Then we'll figure out when I can go back outside to play."

• **Understanding others:** To help your child learn emotional self-control, help him see why other people say and do what they do. When he says "my teacher wasn't fair today," help him see some of the reasons – she didn't see everything that happened, or there were visitors in the classroom and she was busy. And brainstorm with your child: What can we do when someone is being unfair? **Seeing the other person's perspective is an extremely worthwhile life skill for kids to have.** As parents, we shouldn't just automatically take our child's side or the other person's side when we hear the story from our kids. Help your child see the situation from a different point of view. *Having this skill of empathy is a key to controlling our emotions*, the rationality of our reactions, and the ability to get along with each other. These things help a child develop emotional self-control and, eventually, emotional maturity.

6. Guiding Your Child's Social Maturity

ASK YOURSELF: *Is my child friendly toward peers and can she play comfortably with them for an hour or more; does she regularly compromise and take turns; does she know how to handle rejection and teasing; does she have any special friends; do you like the children she's attracted to?*

When children can make friends easily, they enjoy school much more. Most children, by this age, are socially comfortable and able to make friends. But if your child finds friendships a challenge, you can help teach her better social skills.

What social skills would be valuable when children enter kindergarten? *Since children may need help getting along with their peers, look through this list of skills we'd like our children to have and mark the ones you want to help your child with:*

• *Your child is friendly toward others: saying hello, smiling, looking at the person, and able to start a conversation: "Let's sit together at snack time, OK?"*

If she isn't friendly, make sure you're modeling friendly greetings and smiles. At home, role-play greeting others in a friendly way. Lightheartedly teach her about looking at the person. Let her know that when she doesn't answer people and doesn't smile at them, it makes them feel sad and lonely.

• *Your child is polite – saying "please" and "thank you"; saying "excuse me" if she's squeezing past someone; asking nicely if she wants to have a turn with something her classmate is using.*

Make sure you've taught her to be polite. Instead of continuing to ask her, "What's the magic word?" or reminding her to say "please" or "excuse me," try something that will shift the responsibility to her: Clear your throat or say, "Hmm?" Don't keep telling her the exact words to say, because then she doesn't have to remember on her own.

• *Your child speaks loudly enough to be heard, but not too loudly.*

When our children are too loud or not loud enough, let them know how it affects us and others. Too loud may mean it startles you, hurts your ears, and makes you unhappy. Too soft may mean you and she get frustrated because you can't hear her. Give her practice and work out a signal that helps her know to correct her volume.

• *Your child is willing to compromise, negotiate, and take turns (not always having things her way or always giving in). She can play and talk together with friends – true back-and-forth cooperative play – but still needs some adult help to play positively, and she knows how to get help from others if she can't handle what's happening.*

Supervise her peer friendships so she is not consistently dominant or consistently meek. Have playdates at least weekly, but not always with the same child, because children benefit from learning to get along with different friends. Children also need one-on-one playdates to develop social skills because – unlike in school – there's no other child to move on to. On playdates, if your child is having challenges, you should supervise and teach. You should teach both kids right then and have them "practice better behavior," vs. just telling them what they should do differently next time. If both you and the other child's parent are present, see if you can agree on which child's parent is in charge. This is hard to do in practice, but worthwhile. Usually it's "your house – your rules." That way the children will know whom to listen to. *One important way to help your child's social skills is not playing with her in any way that would be a problem if she did it with her peers, such as always letting her go first or decide what to play.* For many examples of how to teach better social skills on a playdate, see *I Want To Make Friends* by this author.

• **Your child is able to express her ideas, views, and preferences to others, and pays attention to others' ideas, views, and preferences.**

If she has difficulty expressing her views or insists her views are of great importance, encourage her to defend her views in your family and gatherings with friends. Don't allow her to monopolize or always have hers be the most important views. Young children's views should not be seen as the most important ones in the family, because then she'll expect to get much of the attention at school.

• **Your child uses words rather than acting out physically when frustrated or angry.**

Use empathy to help her feel that you understand what made her so mad. Practice the words she could say to express her anger. When she's calm, help her understand that parents, teachers, and all schools have a rule that it's never OK to hurt anyone.

• **Your child keeps her hands to herself and doesn't tickle, poke, or roll over on others – basically respects other kids.**

Work on this at home first. If your four- or five-year-

old sits on you without any notice, pulls you by the hand, or treats your body as an extension of hers, point it out and teach her to use her words. If this happens with playdates, teach her the words she should use instead.

• **Your child has some skill in handling rejection from others, such as when kids say, "I don't want to play with you."**

Tell her so she understands why kids may not want to play with her right now. Teach her to suggest a fun idea or to say, "Maybe later."

• **Your child has some skill in handling insults from others, such as when kids say, "You're a crybaby," "You look like a boy," or "You're stupid and everyone knows that."**

Practice this kind of comment at home, helping her understand why someone would say this and how she could respond. An effective, simple response your child can use that doesn't cause the situation to escalate would be, "So?"

• **Your child has some ability to handle teasing, such as when a kid says, "You're supposed to draw a shark, but that looks like a snark."**

There are many ways to respond to this, such as, "I like my snark!" But if her reaction shows that she's sensitive, that's likely to make her a further target. You could give her practice being teased a little, gently, at home. This will make her more able to handle things at school, as teachers can't possibly hear or deal with the many, many minor but potentially troublesome comments among the kids.

• **Your child is increasingly better able to see other people's perspectives and not just her own.**

Help her begin to understand why the other person did what he did and why your child did what she did. This is a great social skill.

• **Your child has learned the rules of common games (such as Chutes and Ladders) and accepts that those rules have to be followed.**

Teach her the rules of the common board games, card games, and playground games. She's now old enough for us to stop bending the rules. Teach her some calming mantras – "It's not that bad. It's not that bad." Tell her what you tell yourself when you don't win. If you only think of winning, it's hard to have fun when you play

games. Help her think in terms of first and second – not winner or loser.

• *Your child accepts that there are rules in and out of the class, such as immediately putting your pencil down when the teacher tells you to, and not running or shouting in the halls.*

Be sure to teach her the rules of your family and community, such as not running in stores.

• *Your child is starting to have some special friends and is attracted to children who are well-enough-behaved, nice kids.*

Pay attention to the kinds of kids she is becoming friends with. Many kids like to have special friends – often those with similar interests, temperaments, and activity levels. *If you're unhappy with the children your child is attracted to, try to get to know them and their parents better.* If the children really are bad influences on each other, you'll want to get the teachers' help with separating them more and to diplomatically talk to your child about your concerns. Ask the teacher to suggest some other children in the class who might be more appropriate playmates. You can teach her how to see the differences between children who care about her and the others who do things they shouldn't and try to get her to join in. *Tell about some of your peers as a child and your struggles trying to have friends who were really the right ones to be with.*

• *Your child is better at knowing right from wrong than when she was younger, but still needs supervision and guidance.*

By this age, children usually know they shouldn't take things from school, call others names, hit them, or break things. Most know right from wrong, but a child may still get out of control when other kids act up, or a child may lie about whether she did something she shouldn't have. Continuing to teach your child right from wrong is important. Talk to your kids about times you wanted to do (or did) something that wasn't the right way to behave. Discuss why it wasn't right and what was the right thing to do. *Suggest what she can say to herself when she feels like doing something she shouldn't. Ask if she has other ideas. Explain why people sometimes do wrong things. Talk about what to do when that happens.* Should your kids try to stop the wrong behavior, go get an adult, or just wait till they see you? Make sure

you tell your kids, "I'm not as bothered about what you did as I am that you lied to me when I asked you about it." Some children find it much easier than others to do the right thing. We need to be watchful and able to guide them as our kids grow and experience new possibilities for right vs. wrong behavior.

SECTION TWO
GUIDING YOUR CHILD: FOUR THROUGH FIVE YEARS (PRE-K)

7. Your Child's Speech and Language Readiness

ASK YOURSELF: *Does my child understand and remember information and directions? And is he able to be understood by others, wait for his turn to speak in a group, speak loudly enough, answer questions, and explain things well?*

In order to participate fully and successfully in kindergarten, a child has to understand what's being said (receptive language) and speak so others can understand him (expressive language). Although most children are sufficiently skilled in both aspects of language, this section will help you know if that's true for your child and how to help him if needed.

Receptive Language

Teachers in kindergarten expect children to:

★ listen and understand when others talk to them

★ do what the teacher/other adults ask of them (begin their work, get in line)

★ be quiet when others are talking, when the class is working, and when walking in the halls

Give your child enough experience at home with the following ways to be a good listener:

• Make sure you *read him lots of stories* – several a day – so he learns to listen and feel positive about books and reading. Ask him questions to see how well he understands what you're reading to him.

• Regularly *explain things* to your child and be sure he understands them. (You can have him repeat them back to you if you have doubts.)

• **Give him directions** and make sure he is doing what you ask. Some of your directions should have multiple steps so he learns to remember them on his own and carry them out. (For example, "Please put your socks in the laundry basket, change your shirt, and bring your box of markers downstairs.")

• Teach him to be **quiet** at home **when you ask him to** (such as when you're talking on the phone.)

• Give him experience as part of a group or family gathering where he has to **wait his turn to speak** and has to **listen to what the others are saying** and not just tune out. Listening patiently while paying good attention is a very important skill for children and adults.

Occasionally, children are delayed in receptive language (understanding what's said). Almost always, parents notice this because their child frequently doesn't seem to get what they said even when it's something he'd want to hear. This "receptive language" delay is different from when we joke about our child's selective hearing – he hears when you ask if he wants a cookie, but not when you tell him to pick up his toys. If you suspect a receptive hearing problem, ask your pediatrician to check this out and, if needed, refer your child for an audiology evaluation.

Expressive Language

The other important aspect of speech and language development is being able to express himself well enough in words. A red flag is if you, his parents, have difficulty understanding him. There are only a few sounds or sound combinations that are still hard for children by kindergarten age, so **kindergartners should be easy to understand**. If you and his teachers have to regularly ask him to repeat himself and other kids ask, "What did he say?" it would be worthwhile getting a speech evaluation. Adults such as teachers usually have the patience to try and understand what your child is saying, but kindergartners don't.

Kindergarten teachers expect children to communicate in the following ways:

★ be comfortable talking about what's happening in their life

★ respond to or initiate conversation with peers

★ speak loudly enough to be heard, but not so loud that it's annoying

★ raise their hands and then wait their turn to share information, ask questions, or answer questions in a group

So it's important that your child get enough experience at home in the following ways so he can be a good communicator:

• getting your full attention at times so **he can tell you** about what he's experiencing

• **asking questions** like who, what, where, but also how and when.

• **answering** your questions

• **waiting for his turn** with other family members and then being able to hold the attention of the others as he expresses himself – easy to do at dinner

• having friends to talk to and play with and **making sure the way they talk to each other is acceptable.** Taking turns while speaking is important with adults, sibs, and peers.

Some children entering kindergarten still have small vocabularies, use the tense incorrectly ("he runned away"), have difficulty finding the right word, get their words out of order, don't use plurals ("there were a lot of mouse"), forget what they wanted to say, or stutter. Your pediatrician can make a speech and language referral for your child. In many school districts, the special education department provides evaluation and therapy services to children beginning at age three years. Most children make better progress if special education help begins early, before starting kindergarten. For additional guidelines and tips, go to the website of the American Speech and Hearing Association at www.asha.org.

8. Your Child's Fine and Gross Motor Readiness[4]

ASK YOURSELF: *Does my child play happily indoors and outdoors? Does she build, do puzzles, use crafts materials, and color within the lines? Is she using a pencil? Is she printing her name, drawing shapes, and making pictures? Do I wonder if she has enough fine motor skill to be ready for kindergarten? Does she run, climb, jump, and hop as well as other kids her age?*

This section will help you understand what level of fine and gross motor skills a child should have by kindergarten. Your child may love the outdoors and have great gross motor skills but may be less interested in indoor-type, fine-motor activities, or vice versa. If you have one or the other, it would be valuable to **help your child also find enjoyment and success in the areas she is less interested in.** You may get some resistance. We want to give our kids opportunities and encouragement so they're prepared for school, but not make them feel forced or judged. Every parent is aware that children have individual differences, which we want to appreciate.

Both kinds of motor skills will be needed in kindergarten. For example, the teacher may ask the children to get in line and gallop around the field, then jump five times and hop three times. Or your child may need to color inside the lines, cut, and glue. If she is inexperienced in these skills, she may not be able to keep up with the group.

There are many ways a young child can develop more interest and ability in motor skills. In this section, mark the ones you think you need to encourage more. As needed, help her enjoy them. You can do them with her, have her do them with friends or siblings, or do them to music. Make sure she feels successful. Try to avoid always being better at these activities than she is. It's useful for the young child to have most of the following opportunities.

Fine Motor Skills

Play – Blocks; Legos; puzzles; pegboards; lacing cards; card and board games; cars and trucks; crafts materials like Play-Doh; coloring, painting; gluing and cutting; sand, dirt, and water play; ball play; and working with tools (such as hammers and screwdrivers)

Self-care and helping out – Dressing (and undressing), including buttons and zippers; practice putting on shoes and beginning to try tying laces (even though Velcro is widely used); eating with a fork and spoon; using a knife for spreading; being able to cut soft foods such as bananas or zucchini; closing and opening jars and containers; closing and opening zip-seal bags.

Writing and drawing

Continue to encourage practice in all these areas:

• Provide **crayons and markers**. Although markers are easier to use, you shouldn't **always** have them available, because your child's hand strength may be compromised. Teachers usually use crayons more than markers.

• Encourage her interest in **coloring books**. Show her how to color inside the lines as much as possible and how to fill in the picture.

• **Teach** your child the **tripod grip** so she's using three fingers to hold and support her pencil – typically thumb, index finger, and middle finger. If your child is having trouble with this in the pre-K year, get help from the pre-K teacher or the upcoming kindergarten teacher. You can also try a molded pencil grip such as the Jumbo Pencil Grip. Also, try Crayon Rocks. You want your child to be able to hold the pencil for several minutes of writing or drawing.

• Use **short or medium-length pencils**, preferably thick ones.

---

4 Fine motor refers to small movements using muscles of the fingers and wrist. Gross motor refers to bigger movements of the large muscles of arms, legs, and torso.

- Teach your child to trace over ∿∿∿ ∿∿∿ and *draw basic shapes* ● ■ ▬ ▲

- Show her *how to erase*.

- Use *dot-to-dot books;* these encourage pencil control to create a picture.

- *Start her on upper-case letters.* Check to see if the school would also like the children to know lower case when they begin kindergarten. (Ask your child's school for a page on how parents should teach children entering kindergarten to form letters.) It's most helpful if you teach letter formation at home the way they do at school. This following website provides specific steps: http://www.kidslearningstation.com/preschool/teach-printing.asp. For example. 𝐀

- Teach your child how to *draw a person*. (Emphasize all the parts of the body that make the picture recognizable as a person.)

- Encourage your child to *draw common images:* a house, a tree, flowers and grass, sky, sun, a cat, a rocketship, cars. (Hang up her art to show her how proud you are of her work.)

- Have her practice *cutting on the lines* and *gluing*.

Gross Motor Skills

- In kindergarten, children will be *expected to sit at their tables, on the floor, and on benches such as at the lunch table.* Some children have trouble sitting on the rug. They may roll around or lie down. Some may have trouble staying on their chairs. Make sure your child has had enough experience at home with sitting for at least 15 minutes at a time when she's playing, drawing, or eating. If she has trouble, make sure that her feet reach the ground where she's sitting, because dangling feet are uncomfortable. If you can't figure out why she can't sit still for about 15 minutes when she's engaged in something interesting, check with the pre-K teacher (or with your child's pediatrician).

- Children will also be asked to *stand in line and walk in line* at school. Kids don't usually have much practice before elementary school with being in a line. If you think she may need practice, find out whether this is expected at preschool and also try it at home.

- Children should have *mastered running and climbing.*

- Children usually have learned to *jump, gallop, and hop* by the time they start kindergarten. These are all fun to practice with your kids using music.

- They should also be able to walk through a crowded room *without bumping into people or obstacles* or tripping on them. (This is often referred to as "a sense of personal space.")

Here are some other gross motor skills for you to check out with your "almost" kindergartner, so she has some familiarity with them:

- Awareness of her own strength and force so she knows *how hard to throw, how hard to hug,* etc.

- The ability to *walk backward.*

- The ability to *pump a swing* with her legs.

- Familiarity with *hopscotch, jump rope,* and *hula hoops.*

- Some competence at *monkey bars* and *rings* (hand over hand).

- Some ability to *catch* and *throw balls.*

- Exposure to *beginning soccer, basketball, baseball,* and *tetherball*, and some *introduction to the rules.*

- Some experience with *two-wheeler bicycles* – some entering kindergartners may be able to ride without training wheels. (If kids don't live where it's flat and safe to bike, they will usually not have had much experience with bikes.)

- Some experience with a *scooter* or *roller skates.*

- The opportunity to try dance, gymnastics, martial arts, etc.

If these motor skills are hard for your child, try to do one or two of these things with her every day for just a few minutes and make it fun. Make sure she begins and ends with success and your smiles and praise. Follow this with an activity of her choice. Include a sibling or friend who could learn with her. Younger sibs age two and up often like to imitate what older sibs are learning. Practicing with her younger sib can build the pre-kindergartner's confidence.

Additional information on motor development can be found through the American Occupational Therapy Association. (Go to www.aota.org and click on "Consumer.") *If you think your child's motor skills are*

significantly behind and she isn't responding to the opportunities and encouragement you're providing, consult with your child's pediatrician. If needed, contact your school district's special education department or a pediatric occupational therapist.

9. Preparing Your Child Academically for Kindergarten

ASK YOURSELF: *Does my child enjoy being read to? Can he answer questions showing he's understanding the story? Is he showing interest in letters and words? Is he making progress writing his first name and other letters? Is he counting past 10 and writing some numbers? Is he drawing trees, houses, etc., and coloring inside the lines?*

Reading to Your Child

Most parents have been reading to their children since they were very little. Reading to your preschooler every day provides that warm, nurturing, and bonding experience that motivates him to love books. Bedtime stories – usually one or two – should be an essential part of the "going to sleep" ritual. (Giving your child a choice between TV or a story is not recommended. When you offer this choice, many youngsters pick TV and then get upset when you won't also read a story.)

When you read to your child, **ask him questions about the story.** Listen and expand – if appropriate – on what he says. **Answer his questions**. Sometimes children just want to relax, cuddle, and be read to, and other times they are eager to ask and answer questions about the story. Both experiences are valuable for children. (Teach your child to wait till the end of the page to ask you questions. This kind of self-control will be expected in kindergarten.)

What Does Your Child Need to Know About Books and About Starting to Read?

Make sure your child knows which is the front and which is the back of the book. Where is the title, which page we start reading on, and what page is next. Read with your fingers below the words some of the time. This helps him see that we read from top to bottom and left to right and what the word you're reading sounds like. See if he can point out to you what order we read the words in, and where the first word on the next line is. All this makes it easier for children to learn to read in kindergarten.

If your youngster seems especially interested and ready to read, you can get recommendations for how to teach him from the pre-kindergarten or upcoming kindergarten teacher. A reliable easy-to-follow program is *The Reading Lesson: Teach Your Child to Read in 20 Easy Lessons* by Michael Levin and Charan Langton (Mountcastle Co., 2002).

Noticing Words

Your child may also start to show interest in the many words in our world, such as on street signs, names on cereal boxes and businesses, and the words he sees on our mail. It is helpful to answer his questions and see what other help he may want as he realizes there is meaning to alphabet letters. For example, at a stop sign, your child says, "What does that say?" When you say "stop," he may start to make the sound of the S but get stuck after that. Help him identify the T. See if he knows the sound – *"tuh"* – and try to help him blend S with *"tuh,"* etc.

Recognizing Alphabet Letters and their Sounds

Start teaching your child to recognize letters. See if your child's kindergarten wants you to teach upper *and* lower case as you introduce each letter. Have fun singing the "ABC" song that most kids have known since age two or three. Use alphabet letter puzzles. After your child knows the first few letters in order, show them out of order and see if he can still identify them. Learning the letters in small groups may make it easier for him to learn the letter names – A, B, C, D, then E, F, G, H, etc.

We want to make this learning fun. Parents can make this process smoother by playing "school" for about 10 minutes a day. *Start and end the "school time" by giving your child something he is successful with.* We want him to remember the time as enjoyable. (Some parents use a tray of sand or shaving cream to help their children make letters, numbers, and shapes with their fingers. This is usually easier than using pencils or crayons, though it's messier!) When he can recognize most of the letters (upper or upper and lower case), help him learn the common sounds the letters make. (See the reference on page 41: *The Reading Lesson*).

Printing His Name and Other Letters

Children entering kindergarten *should know how to print their first name*. They'll need to print their names on their papers many times a day. Depending on what the school tells you, teach your child to print his name in only uppercase letters or both upper and lowercase letters by the beginning of the school year. This is not easy for most incoming kindergartners, so don't expect well-formed letters. Teach your child how to erase. Ask the preschool teacher for advice if your child is especially resistant or unskilled in printing. There is a commonly used approach to teaching children how to form their letters. (If the school doesn't have one it recommends, go to http://www.kidslearningstation. com/preschool/teach-printing.asp to find traceable worksheets for each letter. Pay close attention to the arrows and their order.)

Numbers, Colors and Shapes, and Coloring

Children should be able to count at least to 20, and write and recognize written numbers up to 10. They should be able to put the numbers in order from 1 to 10. Teach your child to count small groups of items – two, five, eight items, etc. Children entering kindergarten should be able to recognize all the common colors. They should also be able to recognize and draw the common shapes: circle, square, rectangle, and triangle. Encourage them to hunt for shapes on signs, in pictures, etc. Help your child draw pictures of things in his world, including pictures of his family. Some children are quick to judge their writing or drawing as not good enough. This can discourage them from trying. Stick to simple versions in *your* drawings.

The book *Get Ready for Kindergarten* by Jane Carole (Black Dog and Leventhal, 2011) is particularly useful for teaching all the basic readiness skills for kindergarten. It has more than 300 pages of useful and colorful worksheets, including the preferred way to teach how to make each letter and number.

Just remember that there is a wide range of skill and interest among children in these basics of reading and writing. Read to your child and help him practice some letter identification and printing – especially his first name, if possible every day. Don't expect perfection. Pencil control takes a lot of practice. You may not see your child forming letters well until first grade. Make it enjoyable and help him feel successful and interested. Adjust your expectations as needed. Children do compare themselves to their classmates in many areas such as schoolwork, friendships, and even athletics. We want to help them be ready for kindergarten so they don't feel they're behind their peers. Kindergarten teachers will teach your children a lot, but they need the children to come in with an introduction to the basics and an attitude of interest, willingness, and excitement. *If we prepare them by teaching what they're capable of learning, they will be motivated to keep learning in kindergarten.*

10. Preparing Your Child for the Structure of Kindergarten

ASK YOURSELF: *Will my child be able to quietly listen when the teacher is teaching the whole class? Will she be able to work on her own doing her assigned classwork? Is she used to raising her hand and waiting to be called on? Can she accept the many transitions from activity to activity and from teacher to teacher?*

If you feel that your child doesn't usually do what you ask, go back and read the section Teaching Your Child to Listen to You and Other Adults (pp. 28-29). Entering kindergartners need to have already learned to do what adults say. In today's kindergarten, the day is three to six hours long, depending on the particular school, school district, or your state's department of education. Currently, across the U.S., four- to five-hour kindergarten days are most common. To be ready for classroom learning, your child needs to be able to be attentive and quiet in a large group. (Fifteen to 30 children are likely to be in her class.) She also has to be able to work independently at her table on her practice pages and booklets, and on hands-on projects.

• **Practicing simple tasks:** You can help her at home by teaching her to listen as you explain tasks to her, such as how to do a simple project or collect a certain number of books. Make sure she can repeat back what you said and that she does what's asked. When she's working on projects, be sure she's on the right track, **but don't sit with her the whole time, because she needs to start getting used to working mostly independently.**

• **Raising her hand:** She needs to be able to raise her hand in class and to handle the frustration and disappointment of not being called on. You can practice hand-raising at home the summer before kindergarten, and having her wait to be called on before she can speak. You can make a "class" of kids using her sibs, stuffed animals, and friends to give her some fun practice. Teach her to tell herself, "My teacher will call on me another time. She can't call on me or everyone every time."

• **Speaking up:** She also needs to know what she wants to say when she's called on, and speak loud enough to be heard. *Guide her into staying on topic and not talking on and on.* When and if she's frustrated because she didn't get to say what she wanted or speak as long as she wanted, you should be empathetic. "It's hard when you didn't get to say what you wanted. We all have to take turns. When I put you to bed, you'll have more time to tell me what you wanted to." Using empathy can help decrease a child's frustration and resulting anger.

• **Helping out at school:** In addition to whole group lessons, most teachers do small group lessons. Some schools have aides to assist the teacher. Many schools encourage parent volunteers. Children benefit from these additional adults in the classroom. Some classes have "centers," where the teacher may have four to five different projects – usually academic – going on at once at different tables. The children move in small groups from center to center, staying at each for about 15 minutes. Parent volunteers are valuable as they help guide the children through these projects and skills.

Volunteering in your child's classroom – if you can find the time – is both helpful and enjoyable for our children and for us. You'll understand your child's school day more fully, as well as what kids her age are capable of. You'll get to know her friends as well as know better how to teach her at home. It will also be easier to talk to her about school. You'll also have a closer relationship with your child's teacher and more understanding of what she has to accomplish.

• **Classroom transitions:** In some kindergartens, the children have specialty teachers for PE, art, music, computer, and library. Transitioning from teacher to teacher can be challenging for some kids. *Even if she has just one teacher, she still will have many transitions from one subject or activity to the next. Make sure that at home, when it's time to transition, such as time to take a bath or get into the car, you don't give her frequent leeway when you ask her to move on to the next activity.* And, of course, make sure she has experience being with sitters and other adults so she can accept being taught by teachers and others in the classroom.

SECTION THREE

GUIDING YOUR CHILD AS KINDERGARTEN BEGINS: FIVE THROUGH SIX YEARS

11. Preparing Your Kindergartner to Be Able to Focus on the Schoolwork

ASK YOURSELF: *Is my child able to ask for help when he needs it but not depend on the adult for too much help? Is he able to get started on his work and keep working on it without an adult next to him? Does he bother other kids when they're working?*

When it's time for independent work, the kindergarten teacher's goal is that the children will get started, stay focused, and complete their work. Not all kindergartners can do that, and teachers expect to help the children become more independent. Most children will ask questions when they're unsure of what to do or when the work is too hard. Teachers try hard to offer help individualized to each child's needs.

Some children also find that working at tables with other children is very distracting. They or the other kids may be talking too much. Some of the kids may be getting attention through being annoying. Teachers will correct those children, explaining that they're not letting their classmates get their work done. Sometimes teachers will move those children to sit near very quiet and/or focused classmates or have them sit away from the rest of the class. Teachers may also put children's names on the board for recurring distracting behavior or start a behavior chart so that they get a star or sticker for controlling themselves. If a child regularly has these issues, the parents typically get daily behavior reports. Teachers have many other ways (within the guidelines/policy of their school) to help the children learn to control their behavior so they and their classmates can accomplish their school work. (Of course, every child has some bad days.)

• **Focusing on work:** *To help your child be a focused learner at school*, there are several things you can do. Be sure he's experienced with following two- or three-step directions. Ask **him** to repeat them to you and then have him carry out the directions **without** your retelling them to him. We want him to pay attention and expect to have to remember the directions. Try asking him to do that again in about five or ten minutes to see if he can still remember and do what you had asked without any extra reminders by you. This is useful because sometimes there are delays in a classroom between when a teacher explains something and when the children are expected to do it.

• **Problem-solving:** If your child asks you or his teacher for help too often, **teach him to become more of a problem-solver**. For example, if his bike is caught in a ditch and he's frustrated, instead of lifting his bike out of the ditch, have him get off the bike and figure out why it won't move and what he can do about it. **You can tell him, "Your bike is stuck. How can you figure out why?"** Then after he sees why it's stuck, ask him what he can do to get it moving again. These are **thought-provoking and useful questions.** If he says he doesn't know, be empathetic about how hard and frustrating it is when his bike won't move, and explain that you'll be right here while he figures it out. Using problem-solving questions with children helps the child gain the ability to work on his own without needing help for every small challenge.

• **Doing the harder tasks:** If your child claims schoolwork is boring or too hard, go back to "What Should Children Do for the Family?" on pp. 31-32. When he helps with family chores, he will come to realize that

there are some "have-tos" every day regardless of whether they are great fun or not.

• **Coping with distractions:** For children who are not used to focusing on schoolwork with many other children near them, see if you can enroll your child in a "preparation for kindergarten" summer program. If that isn't available, enroll him in a class where the teacher expects all the children to follow her directions and work on the same activity. at the same time. And at home, you can have the family all work on a "school-like" project and have someone be distracting. Teach your child to say to that person, "Could you please stop humming?" or "I can't talk now because I'm supposed to be working."

12. What's a Good Daily Routine for Your Kindergartner?

ASK YOURSELF: *Am I sure she's getting enough sleep? How can she get ready for school in the morning without being told repeatedly to hurry up? How much of the morning routine can she do on her own? After school, what does she need to have a balanced day? What should I expect during my child's adjustment to kindergarten?*

• **Time to end naps:** Since your kindergartner probably won't have the time in the day to nap, use the summer to stop any naps she was still taking. In the weeks before kindergarten begins, get her used to reasonable and regular bedtimes. See "What Guidelines at Home Will Help Your Child be Ready to Learn at School," pp. 29-30, for more on sleep and other essentials.

• **Morning routines:** Once she starts kindergarten, make sure you allow enough time in the morning for her to get everything done, usually 45 minutes to an hour. Getting ready for school is often hectic and rushed. *We don't want to stress our kids (and ourselves) by constantly telling the kids to hurry up from the time they get up till they leave for school.* This can really negatively impact their attitude toward school. Overall, it's best to **work with our kids** to make a list that includes pictures and phrases of all that has to be done – such as picking out clothes, getting dressed, eating, and brushing teeth. Children often enjoy adding ideas and decorating their list or poster so it's theirs as well as yours. It helps when our children generate suggestions and understand the reason for the order of things. Help them figure out where to hang it.

• **Morning supervision:** Most kindergartners aren't self-disciplined enough to get ready for school without supervision and reminders. Some parents have their children dress near them while we're dressing or making breakfast, so when they're dressing, etc., we're modeling staying focused. That way, they can accomplish their tasks without so many of the "hurry-ups." *Many children are more willing to keep on task in the morning by working toward having some play time before they leave for school.* If they have time to play, don't allow TV or other electronics, because when it's time to stop they're likely to resist, creating a predictable daily battle. Instead, encourage active play, fantasy play, and so on, with an emphasis on their interests.

• **After-school time:** After school, some playtime and snack time is important. If there's homework – which is not common for kindergartners – try hard to get it done before dinner. Kindergartners are too tired to do all of it in the evening and too young to do all of it alone. Usually we sit with them for some of the time, providing help when they need it, and we stay nearby doing other things during the homework that they can do themselves.

• **Relaxed activities:** After school, it's wonderful for kids to have time to be together with parents to talk, play, and work together on chores (which is more fun than it sounds!); to do some activities on their own; and time to play with siblings, neighbor kids, and playdates. If the kindergarten day is not too long, some outings in the community are always fun. All this can make for a good balance in a day.

• **Getting adjusted:** Kindergartners often find the *first few months of school* very demanding, and many don't have the stamina for after-school activities until they adjust. *Children may be grumpy, irritable, and difficult as they get used to these increased expectations*. In your planning, remember they've been in a group all during the school day, with lots of necessary teacher demands and probably peer pressure, so try and *balance that with enough individual time and less pressure in the rest of the day.* Allow enough time for an unrushed bedtime routine with bath, stories, and time to chat. Children especially love to share meaningful experiences from their day with their parents at bedtime.

13. Working with Your Child's Kindergarten Teacher

ASK YOURSELF: *How can my child and I have a good working relationship with his kindergarten teacher? What if our child's teacher is concerned about his learning or behavior?*

In the early fall, schools hold back-to-school night, and later in the fall, you get feedback at your parent-teacher conference. *It's best to establish a partnership with the teacher so our child feels that both his teacher and his parents know what's going on in his world.* Keep the teacher informed about any stresses at home such as parents traveling, sickness, death of someone close, etc. Find out the best way to communicate with the teacher. Many prefer e-mail.

It's common for teachers to notice areas where our children need some additional help. These could be academic or behavioral. They may ask us to work with our children in these areas (such as learning to raise his hand before he talks or learning more alphabet letters). *Occasionally* teachers may feel that despite all your efforts, and theirs, more help is needed, and may suggest a learning or behavior evaluation. Public schools can usually provide these assessments at no cost to us (and private schools can recommend an evaluation specialist). Your child's pediatrician can also recommend a specialist.

When a teacher feels our child has a noticeable problem, we can easily get defensive at what sounds like criticism. We may strongly disagree, blame her for the problems, and even want to change teachers or schools. Try very hard not to go down that road. Consider the teacher's recommendations seriously, understanding that she wants your child – as you do – to have a successful year. *Ask enough questions so that you know exactly what the problems are and when they occur. Have you observed what the teacher is talking about?* Arrange an initial conversation with the appropriate specialist to determine if you want to proceed. Remember, help is more effective when it starts sooner rather than later. Finally, do not criticize your child's teacher in any way that your child will overhear. It is nearly impossible for your child to learn from a teacher you don't respect, and it will make being at school a negative or at least an ambivalent experience for him. We shouldn't do that to our kids.

CONCLUSION

Kindergarten is a major milestone for every child and his or her parents. As parents, we hope that our children are well prepared socially, emotionally, and academically for kindergarten with all that we and their preschool teachers have done. We hope that our children will enjoy school, be good learners, have friends, and behave well.

The story for children and the parent guidance section in this book will **ensure that you don't overlook anything that will make your child's adjustment to kindergarten as smooth as possible**. The story will help you feel more confident that you know how to address your child's questions and possible anxieties. And you'll be more sure that you know how to work with your child as he or she begins this promising entry into the "big kids'" world of formal education. Our youngsters are starting to grow up. That's both exciting and challenging for them and for us. Being informed and prepared will help a lot in making kindergarten a good year for the whole family.

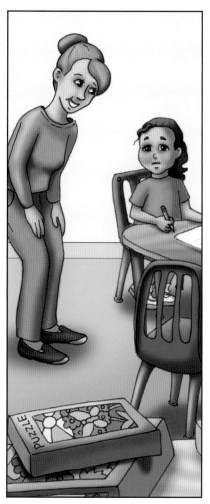

B. ANNYE ROTHENBERG, Ph.D., *author*, has been a child/parent psychologist and a specialist in child rearing and development of young children for more than 25 years. Her parenting psychology practice is in Redwood City, CA, and she is a frequent speaker to parent groups. She is also an adjunct clinical assistant professor of pediatrics at Stanford University School of Medicine and consults to pediatricians and teachers. Dr. Rothenberg was the founder/director of the Child Rearing parenting program in Palo Alto, CA, and is the author of the award-winning book *Parentmaking* (Banster Press, 1982, 1995) and other parenting education books for parenting guidance professionals. Dr. Rothenberg is the author of all the books in this award-winning series for preschoolers, kindergartners, and their parents: *Mommy and Daddy Are Always Supposed To Say Yes ... Aren't They?* (2007), *Why Do I Have To?* (2008), *I Like To Eat Treats* (2009), *I Don't Want To Go To The Toilet* (2011), and *I Want To Make Friends* (2012). She is the mother of one grown-up son.

BONNIE BRIGHT, *illustrator,* is achieving her lifelong goal of illustrating children's books. As a young girl, growing up in the mountains above Malibu, CA, Bonnie would create tiny story books about the size of your thumbnail. She also has a lifelong love for volleyball, as the daughter of two Olympians, and she herself has competed at a high level. When she was offered a scholarship to play volleyball at UC Santa Barbara in 1984, she jumped at the chance to combine her two passions: volleyball and fine arts. She later studied illustration at Cal State University, Long Beach. Since then, Bonnie has illustrated many books, including *I Love You All The Time*, *The Tangle Tower, Surf Angel*, and *Jenny's Pets.* Bonnie strives to make each book better than the last and to achieve her ultimate goal of bringing her imagination to life. You can visit her website to see more examples of her work: ***www.brightillustration.com***

ACKNOWLEDGEMENTS

The author is extremely grateful to **SuAnn and Kevin Kiser** for their continuing and outstanding critiques and collaboration on the children's story and to **Caroline Grannan** for her thorough and excellent editing of the parents' manual. **Cathleen O'Brien** has again shown her terrific creativity and talent in the book design she has achieved. **Bonnie Bright's** work as an illustrator has been the best and we look forward to our future collaboration.

Many colleagues were willing to spend time providing thoughtful suggestions and reviews of the children's story and the parent guidance section. We are most grateful for the time and efforts of: **Christine Shales, MPA, Principal, Merry Moppets Preschool** and **Belmont Oaks Academy**, Belmont, CA; **Pauline Warren, MA, LMFT, Lower School Counselor, The Harker School**, San Jose, CA; **Mary Ann Zetes, MD, Pediatrician, Altos Oaks Pediatrics**, Los Altos, CA; **Barbara Fourt, MA, OTR, Occupational Therapist, Fourt Therapy Associates**, Menlo Park, CA; **Jan Buchwald, MA, CCC, Speech and Language Pathologist**, San Carlos, CA; **Lisa Dayeh, Preschool Teacher, Woodside Preschool**, Woodside, CA; **Elissa Barrett, Director,** and **Brenda Roberts, Owner, The Roberts School**, Menlo Park, CA; **Moreen Belong, Kindergarten Teacher**, **John Muir Elementary School**, San Jose, CA; **Joyce Ottey, Kindergarten Teacher, Sutter Elementary School**, Santa Clara, CA; and **Lori Kate** and **Gary Smith**, *parents of a first grader*, San Jose, CA; **Allyson Tobias**, *parent of a kindergartner*, Los Altos, CA; and **Bubba** and **Mandy Sandford**, **Pediatrician** and *parents of a kindergartner,* Redwood City, CA.

Be sure to read Dr. Annye Rothenberg's other All-In-One Books.

Mommy And Daddy Are Always Supposed To Say Yes...Aren't They?

A STORY FOR CHILDREN—Like many preschoolers, Alex insists that his parents should always let him have what he wants. Right now! When he plays the parent in a fun role reversal, he begins to see things differently. Alex learns that even when Mom and Dad say no, they still love him ... a lot.
INCLUDES A PARENT MANUAL—*Why don't children get the message about who's the parent?* How to give your child just enough say. How do you deal realistically with the differences between your parenting and your spouse's? This manual includes all this and more.

Why Do I Have To?

A STORY FOR CHILDREN—Sophie wonders why there are so many rules and why her parents want her to follow them. This story teaches your preschoolers just what you want them to learn.
INCLUDES A PARENT MANUAL—Provides the keys to how preschoolers think. It teaches how to make it easier for your children to do what you ask, and offers improved popular consequences and new, more effective ones. *This manual clears up much of the conflicting advice that parents hear.*

I Like To Eat Treats

A STORY FOR CHILDREN—Jack doesn't see why he can't eat whatever he wants. His parents decide to teach him what the many kinds of healthy foods are for. *This story will actually impact your young child's understanding of nutrition.* **INCLUDES A PARENT MANUAL**—*Gives parents realistic guidance on common food questions, such as: How do you get your children to eat food that's good for them? What about picky eaters? How do we change the overeater's habits?* This guidebook will give you many new tools in this important area of lifelong health.

I Don't Want To Go To The Toilet

TWO STORIES FOR CHILDREN — Katie doesn't want to stop playing to go peepee in the toilet. Ben doesn't want to let his poop out in the toilet. *In two motivating and reassuring stories, the children successfully overcome their resistance.* **INCLUDES A PARENT MANUAL** — Learn the child's perspective and how to help when our kids are uninterested, reluctant, and/or fearful. *Parents will discover how to make training happen.*

I Want To Make Friends

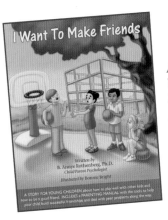

A STORY FOR CHILDREN — Zachary thinks his ideas are the best. He learns how much that bothers the kids. *With the help of his teachers and parents, he becomes a good friend.* **INCLUDES A PARENT MANUAL** — *Learn how to teach your young child good social skills.* Also, what to do if your child is bossy, annoying, or aggressive, or quiet or thin-skinned.

To order these books: visit **www.PerfectingParentingPress.com** where you can order online *or* call (810) 388-9500 (M-F 9-5 ET). These 40- to 48- page books are $9.95 each. Also available at www.Amazon.com.